Hello there friend, my name is Smudge, and if you are sitting comfortably I'd l
it came to pass that some of the creatures we all know and love did come to like roaming around
under the warming rays of the sun, whilst others do now prefer to creep and scurry their way
about in the cold light of the moon.

You see a long, long, long time ago, five friends met up under the shade
provided by the humongous branches of a giant Beechwood tree.

It was early morning and the air was warm and dry.

The crickets chirped, the bumblebees buzzed and the five friends stretched
and yawned, smiled and scratched.

It truly was another glorious summer's day.

Now please my child do let me explain, when I say that this was a 'long, long, long time ago', I should have
said that it was before the time when animals had forgotten how to speak to people, it was even before
people had forgotten how to listen to the animals and it was even long before the time that your
Ma would ever have first met your Pa.

Now, where was I?   O' yes, the five friends...

The five friends would often meet up on a hot summer's day such as this and chat for hours on end,
they would discuss all manner of things, such as *'whether fish go out to do some watering?'*
as them going out *'fishing'* just doesn't sound quite right now does it!

Or they would debate the question of *'Do songbirds read music?'*
as it might seem logical to some that they should.   *Don't you agree?*

But, more often than not, it is fair to say that given the chance these five friends would all
mostly prefer to talk about their two most favourite subjects of all.

"And what were those?"   I do hear you (the owner of a little nose & tiny toes) crow.

Well, the first subject they loved to bicker over was *'Who is the best God of all the Gods?'*
and the second was without fail always, always, honestly always, about *'Food!'*

Sorry my child, what was that?

Oh' I see, I haven't mentioned about the different Gods yet. My apologies...

Okay, well it was all quite simple way back then,
whilst all of the people of the earth worshipped their God and
then did give him many different names, the animals also did do
the same thing for those things that they too gave their great thanks for.

They had a God of Rain, and another of Wind, plus one of Mist and yet
another of Snow, but, during the time I talk of at this moment, on that particularly
fine summer's day, it was the Sun God whose warming rays that they did all very much enjoy.

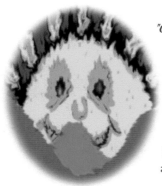

"Good morning my friends!" smiled the **Sun God**, as he glided majestically overhead.

Each of the five friends now did turn their small faces up toward the smiling ball of fire that arched its way across the heavens, whilst he did then continue by saying *"I do hope you've each had a fine nights rest."* The group all nodded contentedly.

For you see my fine small tale-chaser, it must be told that in those days all creatures and all men too, slept when the sun fell and reawakened when he arose once more.

Seeing that his subjects were good and content he did then bid them all fond farewell in the following fashion *"Well I must be going about my business my loyal and ever faithful friends. You all have a lovely day."* this said he then traced his way out across the beautiful pale blue morning sky.

The creatures all smiled at him, waved him their good mornings and then lay lazily back to relish the heartening warmth of his continuing comforting glow through the spread bows and leafy foliage of the mighty Beech tree's shade.

The first to speak was **Tone** the Badger *"I think my favourite of all the Gods, is the **Earth God**, as she always lets me find lots of lovely big fat juicy beetles crawling around on the muddy woodland floor that I may feast upon."*

Tone was a large black and white creature: he lived in a home called a *'Set'* that was dug into the side of a bank of mud, which was snuggled nice and deep within the heart of the unspoilt wooded forest.

He spoke very slowly and had a bit of a rough growl to his voice, but he was in fact a very kind soul at heart.

Next to state her thoughts was **Hoot** the Owl.

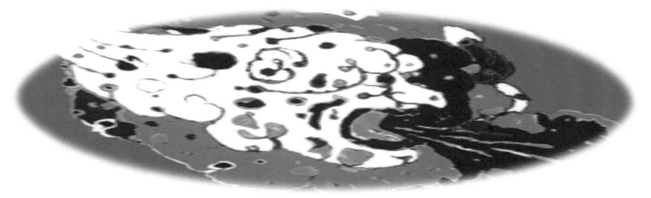

She was viewed by all that knew her, as being
very wise, but also for being a little bit of a snob.

For it was Hoot who lived in the hollow in an ancient Oak tree,
high, high up amongst the top most branches of the wooded forest.

It was probably because she could look down upon all of the others from her lofty perch, that
maybe she felt she was a tiny bit cleverer than the rest of them, not that she would ever
tell them that though, as that, well, it just wouldn't be at all proper now would it.

Hoot had listened very carefully to Tone: she ruffled her feathers of orange and brown
and then decided to plainly speak her mind in answer to his choice of God to praise.

But, my truly fine friend, you must have guessed by now that dear old Hoot the Owl
would of course have to have a very different opinion to that of Tone the Badger.

"I must say..." she trilled and each of the other four
friend's heads all then turned in her direction.

Hoot now preened her fine feathers as the others prepared for her to continue, but she would only do this after an
appropriately long pause, just to ensure that the assembled group were all paying attention to her and her alone.

*"...In my eyes, the **God of the Wind** is second to none.*
As without her, I could not swoop down on all those succulent little field mice now could I!"

Hoot was after all a creature of the wing and therefore could hardly
be expected to choose any other God now could she?

Not to be left out, or even worse be out done in the having-an-opinion stake,
Fluff the Arctic Fox then hastily added *"Everyone knows that the **God of Snow** is the finest of all the Gods. Is it not he, who shows me the tracks to where all the fattest rabbits hide?"*

Fluff was a creature of the cold and lived in a small cave that was high up on the lonely snow capped mountain, which itself sat very deep inside the wooded forest.

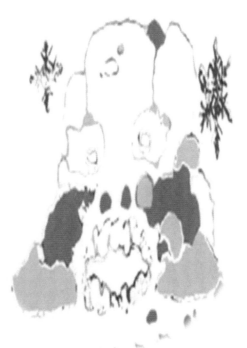

He wore a fur coat as white as white could be and loved nothing more than being on the trail of a tasty fat rabbit: he licked his lips at the thought.

"Now if only I had a bunny in my tummy at the moment, I'd be a very happy fox" continued the wide ginning Fluff.

The subject matter now shifted, as it nearly always did, to the group of five's second most favourite topic in the whole wide world, the subject of... *food!*

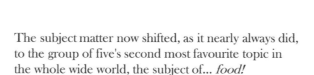

"Worms would be good" said Tone as he scratched at his thick coat of black and white fur.

"Yuck!" Fluff choked at the idea of chewing on slimy earth wrigglers.
"A nice big fat juicy chicken would be better" Fluff thought out loud as he licked his lips.

"Only the Sun God has those Fluff and you know that they're his pride and joy!"
snapped a very flustered Hoot as she ruffled her feathers
in a grand show of her displeasure at the idea.

"It was just an idea that's all, keep your feathers on... Hootie!" chuckled Fluff:
for he knew just how much calling Hoot by her nickname of *'Hootie'* would really quite annoy her.

Hoot stared wide-eyed at the young fox, thoroughly amazed at his cheek.

"It would be good if we could catch ourselves one of those clucking hens though Hoot"
said Tone in his best gravely throated voice, trying to ease some of the tension that everyone else now felt.

"Not so good if we got caught though Tone!" Hoot replied, still shocked at the suggestion.

Then from totally out of the blue came *"I like the **Rain God** the best"*,
this squeaky comment was added to the general ebb and flow of the day's
conversation by a most timid character named **Spike** the Hedgehog, who was
not only the group of five's youngest and therefore most junior member,
but he was also the smallest of our very hungry band of plotters.

Now I must add that this little chap Spike was a creature of leaf piles and hedgerows,
where he wandered around quite freely, choosing to never stay too long in any one spot.

And dearest reader of my story it must also be said that he was feeling very left out of the group's banter at that moment, for although he often imagined what their eggs might taste like, Spike did not truly fancy the idea at all of ever eating the actual chickens from whence the said eggs came.

At this point your old friend Smudge must now tell you that suddenly a fifth and final voice entered the slightly heated vocal sparring match which had broken out amongst our feathered and furry bunch of five friends.

This new voice said in a very harsh and quite rudely dismissive manner *"O' do be quiet young Spike!"* it was a cruel order that was hissed at the poor young bush-pig by a very bossy fellow named **Slink** the Cat.

*"We all know the **God of the Mist** is the one who helps me creep up on all those lazy sparrows"* said this fine figure of feline fortitude, as he rolled onto his back and pawed at a passing butterfly.

For Slink was a creature of cunning and as such he was just as happy around people as he was around these other animals.

Roaming the forest in search of lunch was not an option, not for Slink: no, no, no, not whilst he could choose to lap milk from the saucer of man.

"So, my dear old friend Fluff, do please tell me more about these chickens of the Sun God" said this cunning cat called Slink, with his mouth already watering at the thought.

"As I was saying..." Fluff the Fox enjoyed the chance to finish what he'd been saying
"The only problem about feasting like a God is..." the fox paused,

"Yes?" pressed Slink, as he preened his whiskers.

"...Only the Sun God has both the chickens and the eggs"
Fluff finished speaking with his voice held in an almost whisper.

Meanwhile Slink's sneaky brain had started to hatch a daring plan,
and it must be said that it would be a very sly and rather naughty one too,
a plan that he hoped, if all went well, could soon see him enjoying a very fine chicken dinner.

I should point out that now that Fluff had said those words, Slink felt very safe, after all if his scheme did not
work out as planned, well then he could just pass on the blame by saying it was all Fluff's idea now couldn't he!

So, most loved and cherished readers of my bedtime tale,
with his plan hatched freshly in his own mind, the sneaky Slink
began recruiting a band of fellow night time coop-raiders to his cause.

For it was Slink who would outline a method to raid the Sun God's
chicken-house by which they could all obtain a fine feed of nice
fresh 'poached' chickens and glorious golden 'borrowed' eggs.

Slink then explained that they would *"All need to be involved, if their plan was going to work"*
and with his group of fellow conspirators all gathered in close he weaved his sneaky spell over each of them.

"Before we can even start, my dear sharp eyed Hoot, you'll need to be our lookout..." said the now rather
excited Slink *"...Tone you will have to use all of your wonderful muscles and strength, to dig us a way in
under the fence that stands around the Sun God's chicken-coop."*

He then stopped speaking just for a moment as couldn't help himself as he purred with a knowing smile,
because just as he well understood how to fuss around the legs of man to get the best scraps
from his table or a lovely warm bowl of cream in front of toasty hot fireplace, now
he was happy to play to both the owl and badger's own ever growing egos.

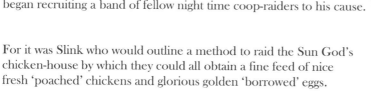

"Then, when the fence is broken open, Spike can quietly scurry in and roll out the eggs one at a time."
Slink continued: deliberately ignoring the worried looks on the other animals faces.
"Once we have enough eggs for all of us, Fluff you'll rush in and grab us
a couple of the fattest, juiciest chooks you can find!"

As Slink explained this part of his devious idea,
he could not help but flash his most wicked grin, but it was also at this point
that a muffled gasp was let out by both Tone and Spike, and even the normally unflappable
Hoot gave a very shocked ruffle of her feathers at the thought of carrying out such a terribly hazardous action.

Yes, my eager wordsmith, it was indeed Hoot who cried out first, as she still looked on at him in amazement
"But Slink, where exactly are you whilst all this goes on?"

Slink was ready for just such a question
"I will of course be doing the most dangerous job of all…"
he hissed contemptuously *"…for it is I, who will be talking to the Sun God himself!"*

All of the other creatures felt their eyes widen and their jaws drop as the cat continued, "Yes *it is I alone, who*
will be keeping him from catching you doing your jobs, and, if I say so myself, it will be at great personal risk,
for it will be I and I alone who will be distracting him, so that each of you can do your task quite safely."

After a short stunned silence there came a brief round of applause and then this comment
"Oh' you are so brave Slink" which was called out by young Spike: who now really wished
that he too had the great courage of his new hero and ever so clever 'friend' Slink the Cat.

The others all nodded in agreement; all except one that is, for it was the wise old owl Hoot,
who wasn't so sure that her chum the cat was being completely truthful, as she sat alone in her silence.

So it was without further ado that the five friends did set out that very night on their most naughty of naughty
adventures, but alas, as is often the case with very naughty, naughty plans, those that plot them
can so often come quite disastrously and deservedly unstuck.

Later that evening, once Slink had made his way to the darkened home of the Sun God, the *Oh-so-brave* cat did find himself all of a quiver, for he, much like all the rest of his merry band, did not exactly 'like' this time of the day very much at all.

You see my friend (of wide eyes & rather short legs) I must tell you that it was in that hour of the night just before the dawn that he now found himself: you may even know the one, it is that hour in which Santa calls and Tooth Fairies lift pillows, it is the loneliest one that always feels the longest and the most dark and miserable, and it is also when it's still very, very cold outside and can even feel just a little bit scary.

This was the hour where you could not even see the whiskers on the side of your face, it was a time when even the warmest of feathers or the cosiest of fur could freeze and stiffen and with only the gloomy half light of the waning moon to see by, which everyone knows doesn't even allow you to see beyond the fog of your very own breath properly, Slink was now feeling more than just a tad nervous.

For the moment Hoot sat perched up on high in the branches of a nearby Ash tree and kept her tired eyes fixed firmly upon the eastern horizon, from which direction she knew the Sun God, being a creature of habit himself, did always liked to start his early morning stroll.

By this moment Tone had long finished digging his hole by the chicken mesh fence and Spike was stealthily rolling the last of the golden eggs out from under the coop's badger busted wire: Slink meanwhile had just spotted the awakening Sun God as he yawned his first rays of light for the coming day.

Being the confident friend of man and a chum to all creatures, Slink casually meandered his way over to warm his frozen paws in the presence of the Sun God, using the same cunning smile that so often earned him the cream from a human's milk jug.

The cat purred his greeting to the bright and wise one *"Good morning O'glorious God of the heavens."*

Not a million miles away at that very moment Fluff had decided now was the best time for him to make his move and as quick as a flash he disappeared through the hole in the fence that had been provided by the badger's powerful claws, then, coming up from under the mesh, he emerged inside of the chicken-coop.

"Slink, my creature of man, what ever brings you to my door whilst it is still so chill and dreary of an early morning hour?" questioned the somewhat bemused and curious Sun God.

But before the cat could even muster a clever answer to the God's question a loud crowing call shattered the morning's eerie silence, renting its way through the misted air and splitting the ears of all who might have heard it.

"My Rooster!" bellowed the Sun God.
"Your what?" gulped a stunned Slink.

Slink however was to hear no answer, for the Sunny-One was already blazing a trail as he made his way across the farmyard toward his chicken house, arriving just in time to see an equally shocked looking Fluff exiting from beneath the wire with two of his fattest and most juicy prized hens gripped firmly between his bloodied teeth.

As a shower of hen feathers
fluttered gently to earth
"Cockle-doodle-do!"
screamed out the rooster.

None of the group of friends had ever seen a sight quite like it. The still crowing bird, with its ear piercing shriek of alarm, wore a crown as red as its master's glowing face and bore long streaming tail feathers, which were just as golden and burned as brightly as the Sun God's own rays of light on a midsummer's afternoon.

*"Meet the herald of my coming you rascals.
Hear the call of my passage through the sky!"*
the Sun God now roared at the quaking group of felons.

"So, I see that my good 'friends' Fluff, Tone and Spike, have all come to visit me as well!"
said the Sun God and as he shouted he burnt as bright an orange colour as was never seen before.

"O' yes, our most favoured God of all things bright and beautiful"
the plotters all now chorused as if with one terrified voice.

"And who do we have there, hiding amongst the branches of my tallest Ash tree?" the Sun God quizzed.

Hoot nearly fell from her roost on high when she realised that she too had been spotted,
from where she now cringed she too spoke *"It is I, Hoot, most illustrious one."*

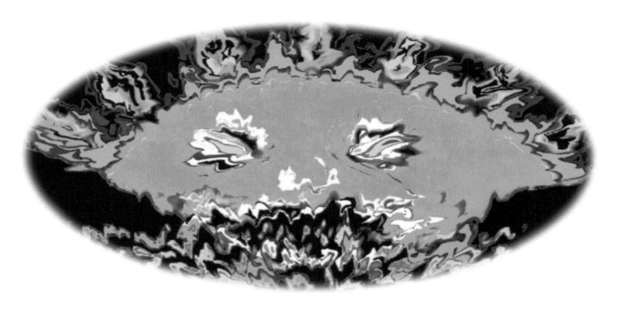

"Slink, come now and join your fellow conspirators" the Sun God ordered
as he did glow a crackling burnished red across the morning's gloom.

Slink let out a choked rasp *"Yes, O' mighty one."*
The five stood cowering, bathed in the Sun God's flaming radiance.

Without missing a beat or with the slightest of hesitation the cat cunningly uttered
"It was all Fluff's idea your worship!" as Slink said this he slowly crept upon his belly and
while fawning his way toward the offended God he began putting his devious escape plan into practice.

"My idea? But, but, you, you..." poor Fluff spluttered, totally lost for words.

"Be quiet you pair!" the Sun God snapped, his face a mask of raging molten lava, *"Now you add insult to injury,
for not only do you come here to my home creeping through the night, intent on stealing my prize birds,
but you do also think of me as a simple fool who can be easily lied to!"*
his temper was obviously way beyond boiling point.

"Well my sneaky wee creatures of the night, the next time you conspire to rob, thieve or steal, maybe you can be made to think twice before committing yourselves to the wickedness of skulking in under your victim's very nose."

The Sun God's rant was now approaching a full head of steam.

But whilst Hoot, Tone, Fluff and young Spike chose to stare meekly at their own paws and claws, Slink had decided to meet the enraged deity's glare eye to eye.

In truth, only the ever arrogant Slink could still think that he could extract himself from the current dilemma he'd now placed himself, and his friends, into.

But by now my good friend you know Slink, and you'll have guessed that he genuinely believed that there was no predicament that he couldn't just try to 'sweet talk' (also known to you and me as a 'lie') his way out of.

"But O' wisest and O' merciful Lord, was I not with you when all of this shabby drama unfolded, was it not I that was coming to warn you, when your Rooster shouted out the alarm?"

The cunning cat purred in his most charming of purrs, whilst merrily selling all of his much beloved and dearest friends down the river, so as to save his own skin: the Sun God now broke into a forced, but strangely still beaming, smile.

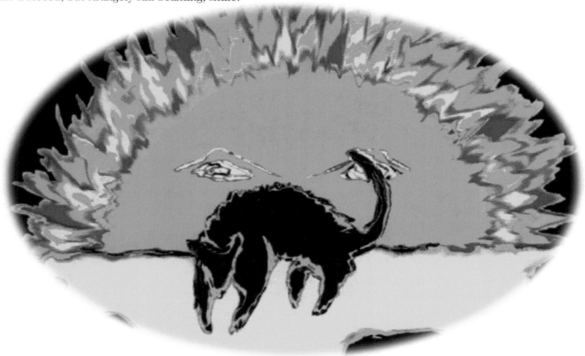

"Slink you have learnt to twist words as well as any man that ever walked beneath my gaze, but if you should choose to utter so much as one more coiled sentence, I promise you this, you and your friends will feel the true heat of my fullest wrath!"

As the Sun God gently seethed, his voice spat white-hot embers across the dawn's now rapidly warming atmosphere.

"But Lord, I only wanted to say..." Slink rudely interrupted:
The cat never was one to know when it was better to hold his tongue and say nothing.

"So be it!" the Sun God commanded his face now a churning pit of fire.

"Tone the Badger, was it not I that heated the gravel that you rolled about on during those lazy hazy days and summer afternoons?" the God stated.

A terrified Tone just nodded his black and white muzzle.

"Then badger I find you guilty of being ungrateful..." the Sun God continued "...not once more will you or your kind enjoy my ray's warmth. You will have a life of living deep in the holes you have dug during my daylight hours, and only at night will you leave the darkest depths of the earth. This shall be your reward!"

Tone merely lowered his head and then he sorrowfully scuttled away, to start a life of being surrounded by the night's murky cold darkness forever more.

"Hoot the Owl, was it not I that warmed the air that provided your wings with lift, so that you could glide across my heavens?"

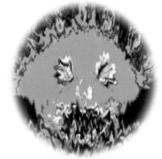

Hoot swivelled her head and then shamefully nodded in the affirmative.

"Then I also find you guilty of being disloyal."
the Sun God said dispassionately.

At this stage in our story I think that you will appreciate that the Sun God was no longer angry about whether his greedy friends had wanted to steal his beautiful chooks.

However, Smudge thinks that his real upset was mainly caused by the simple truth that no one likes to be lied to, now do they!

The Sun God then finally bellowed at Hoot *"A watcher of thieves you are, so now a lookout of the night your offspring shall remain, forever to be destined to call out 'Who-Who?' into the gloom."*

Poor old Hoot shivered, shook her feathers and then she also fled into a life that would find itself ever wrapped around by the cloak of a chilly dusk.

The Sun God now turned his attention to the smallest member of this band of thieves and said
"Spike the Hedgehog, was it not I that warmed your dawn and gave you sips of dew to drink each morning?"

Spike swung his sad little squirming nose from left to right
in a display of his obviously embarrassed agreement.

"Then with regret I find you guilty too, of being self-serving"
the Sun God's sorrow seemed to show through briefly.

*"You and your children's children will forevermore roll
up like an egg upon my coming into the morning sky.
Now go Spike, and look upon my face never more."*

Spike let out the smallest of squeaks and then he too fled into a world of ever lasting night.

"Fluff the Arctic Fox, was it not I that thawed the ice and melted the snow, when you could take no more of the cold on your frostbitten paws?"

Fluff felt his tummy turn to jelly and he had the urge to run, but he just bowed his head low in acknowledgement.

"I also find you guilty, guilty of being both cruel and greedy" the Sun God went on *"...You and your kin will forever more be stained as blood red as the feathers of my poor innocent chickens, you will be pursued by hunters whenever you fall under my path and from this day forth you shall enjoy my favours no more!"*

Fluff let out a sorrowful howl that ended in a yapping whimper as he gazed at his new crimson coat, no longer would he preen his white fur mantle: instead he tucked his brush tail between his hind legs and fled into the deepest darkest corners of the forest, no longer to play unseen on the snowy peaks of his mountainous homelands.

Finally the Sun God turned his attention toward Slink.

"Slink the Cat, was it not I that provided you with the warmth of my light by which you hunted and played?" Slink just looked at the Sun God, defiantly awaiting his fate.

"I find you guilty, of both arrogance and dishonesty" the Sun God stated, the gravity of which was etched upon his glowing features.

"From now until the termination of time itself, O' cunning and lying one, not ever again will you and any of your like walk for long beneath my path, for now you shall all evermore sleep through my most glorious hours."

Slink listened to the Sun God's words and then turned to make hastily away from the scene of his now disastrously failed crime.

"Leave-not yet sad *Slink*, for though you are also to be a creature of the night from this day forth, for you I also assign another punishment, as from this day hence you shall not be free of your tie to man, for it is he who will take you to task and constantly watch over you and ensure that you and your kind are reprimanded should you ever dare to stray again."

After letting out a long loud wailing cry, at last ... *Slink too slunk away into the gloom!*

And so it was to come to pass that Slink, and all his kind thereafter, felt the strangest of urges and did thenceforth decide to forego their freedom and always return to the dwelling place of man and just as the Sun God had promised, it has been true that cats forevermore do now laze their way through the very best part of the day.

Thus my tale is finally told, my most loved and cherished reader

So, now you can relate the facts you've learned to anyone that might ever care to ask you ...

Why do some creatures only become truly awakened at night?

Why do roosters create havoc when the sun rises?

Why do badgers live in holes in the ground?

Why do owls shout 'Who-Who'?

Why do hedgehogs curl up in a ball?

Why do foxes wear such crimson red coats?

And most importantly of all: why is it that my cat is so darn lazy?

You see my most curious and precious child it was all the fault of a naughty cat named Slink and the will of the Sun God... a very, very, very long time ago...

Now child you know the truth ...

as Smudge tells it ...

don't you ...

well, don't you ? !

Smudge's
Picture Gallery

Why don't you have a try at colouring in my face?

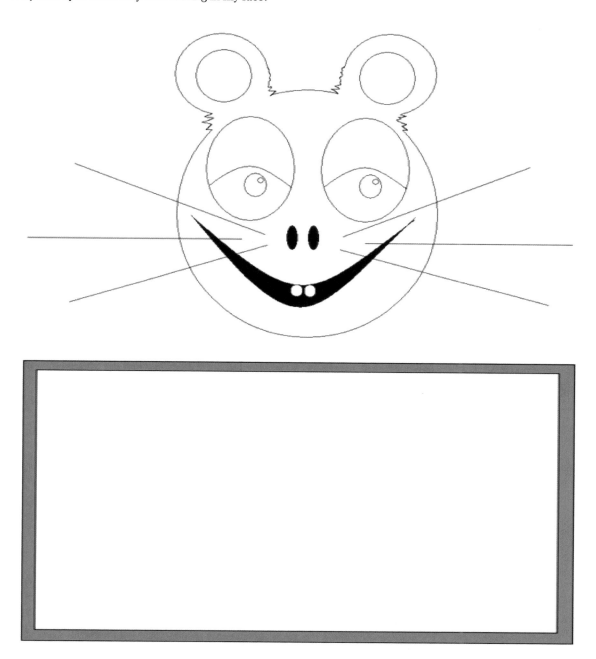

...Or you could even try to draw your own picture of me!

Smudge's
Interesting Creature Facts

Did you know that scientists now believe that
chickens are descended from dinosaurs?

Do you think that you could draw a dinosaur
for your new friend Smudge please?

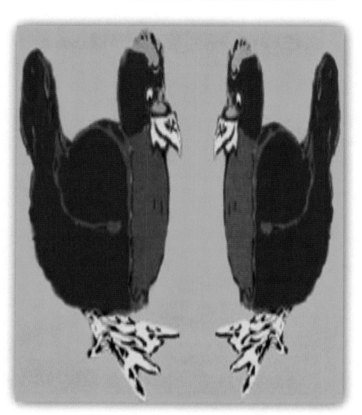

Did you know that just like the chickens
in our story dinosaurs were born from eggs?

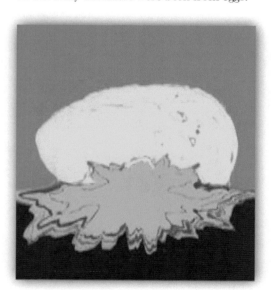

What other creatures do you think might be born out of eggs?
Write their names in this box below please.

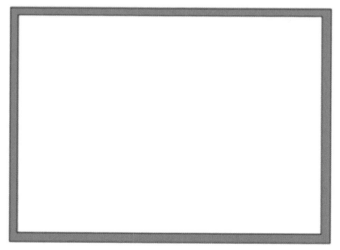

Below are our five friends and their favourite Gods; can you remember who preferred who?

Draw a line to who you think goes with whom: I've already done one to help get you started!

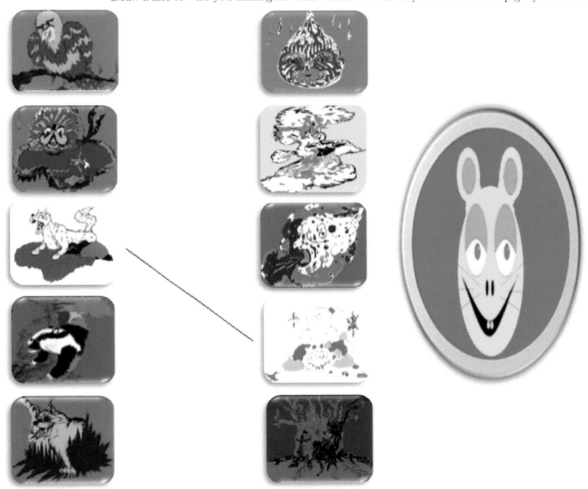

And what was it that you think made the Sun God the most annoyed...
Him having had his prize chooks stolen from him? Or was there something else he thought even worse?

How many times does my picture appear in this book?

When the very angry Sun God tells Slink off, who is it that the naughty cat tries to blame?

What reason did Spike give for choosing his favourite God?

What type of tree did our five friends all sit under at the beginning of my tale?

Who was the first God to be mentioned in our story?

Smudge's
Cartoon Workshop

Hey my friend, it looks like my face has fallen to pieces, would you like to see if you can copy my mouth, eyes and ears into the box at the bottom of the page and put me back together again please?

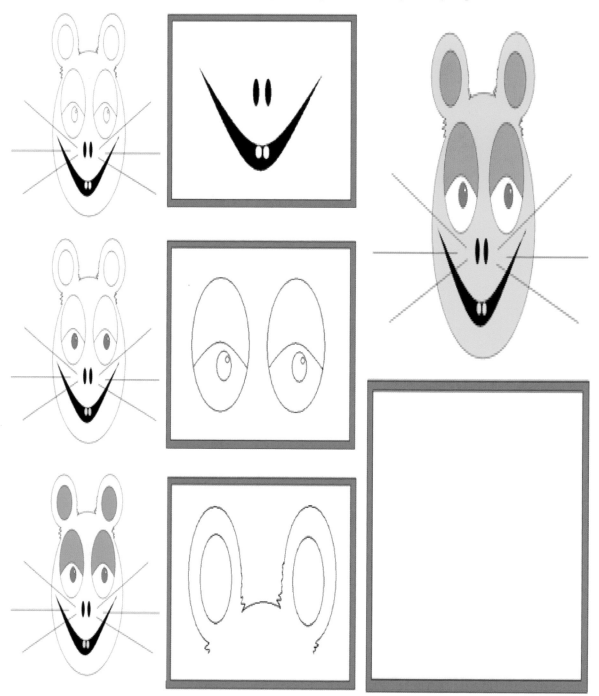

Phew, thanks!   That's much better, I can see that you're quite an artist my friend.

A Message from Smudge and his Friends

The sun can be very good for us, but only if we make sure that we don't stay out in it for too long...

Smudge says
"Always make sure that you put on plenty of sun cream before you go out to play on hot days!"

Splashing around in cool water with your friends can be truly great fun, especially on the very hottest of summer days...

Slink says
"Although water can be great to lark about in, it can also be dangerous: you should never go near it without a grown-up!"

Watching creatures like our little friend Spike can bring you hours of joy and help you to learn lots of fun things about nature...

Tone says
"Please remember that we wild animals do not like to be disturbed and a good rule is to 'look' at us, but never to 'touch' us!"

Climbing a tree can be a huge adventure and if you're lucky enough to live near a forest you'll know how magical they are...

Hoot says
"Do be careful when you go clambering up a tree, as you may not just fall and hurt yourself, you might also scare me too!"

Smudge's
Loving Dedication

This book is dedicated to its author's mother

Mrs Joan Mary Axe

For it was she that sat tirelessly for hours on end
in my childhood, making up tale after tale
and feeding my craving for
bedtime stories

Although eventually robbed of her incredible imagination
and life itself by the ravages of Alzheimer's disease
she remains my rock, my strength
and my imagination's seed

I love and miss you *Muv'er*, more than you can ever know,
more than I can ever say and more than
any cruel twist of nature can
ever undermine

Neil

xXx

Proof

Made in the USA
Charleston, SC
08 January 2014